SIBLING SPLIT

TROUBLE IN THE CITY

BY M.G. HIGGINS   ILLUSTRATIONS BY JO TAYLOR

STONE ARCH BOOKS
a capstone imprint

Sibling Split is published by Stone Arch Books,
A Capstone Imprint
1710 Roe Crest Drive
North Mankato, Minnesota 56003
www.mycapstone.com

Library of Congress Cataloging-in-Publication Data is available on the Library of Congress website.

ISBN: 978-1-4965-2591-8 (library hardcover
ISBN: 978-1-4965-2692-2 (paperback)
ISBN: 978-1-4965-2700-4 (ebook pdf)

Summary: Now that summer is over and school is beginning, separated siblings Annabelle and Arnie are struggling to cope with the reality of life apart — but when Annabelle comes to her mother and brother's apartment in the city, a lot of repressed emotion suddenly overflows.

Designer: Kristi Carlson
Production: Laura Manthe
Image credits: SunStreet Photo, author photo; Jo Taylor, illustrator photo

Printed in Canada.
009629F16

TABLE OF CONTENTS

Annabelle

My name is Annabelle Beeler, and I'm eleven years old. I love planting vegetables in my garden and watching them grow. I like eating and canning them, too. I would much rather be outdoors doing things — like helping my dad build his Adirondak boat or constructing a bat house for the barn — than sitting in class at school. That's why summer is my favorite time of year.

Arnie

I'm Arnie Beeler, age twelve. I love school. Actually, I love learning about almost anything, which is why the library is one of my favorite places. I especially like birds, and Mom and I watch for them when we jog. My sister, Annabelle, would probably tell you that I'm a know-it-all, but she doesn't complain about it when I come up with facts that help her with her projects.

Arnie

CHAPTER 1
ROOF ACCESS

The book I'm reading on insects is amazing. I had no idea the Hercules beetle can lift 850 times its own weight or that it can grow as long as a man's hand. Even though the book is fascinating, I turn the page and the lines of text blur together as my mind wanders again. I keep getting distracted, thinking about how I'll be starting at my new school in only three days. I'm nervous, especially knowing that my sister, Annabelle, won't be by my side.

I close the book and set it on the side table. I know I should get up and do something, but what? I could jog, but Mom is at work, and I don't want to go without her. The library is only two blocks away, and Mom is okay if I go by myself, but I was just there yesterday.

I wish Annabelle were here. Even though she's a year younger than me, she's much braver than I am. She'd be out exploring the city instead of sitting inside this stuffy apartment all day.

Thinking about Annabelle makes me homesick for the farm. Luckily, Mom got cell phones for both Annabelle and me. She said they would help us stay in touch. Mostly I think she got them because she feels guilty she and Dad separated and Annabelle and I don't live together anymore. I pull my phone out of my pocket. I already texted Annabelle this morning, so this time I call.

She answers right away. "Hey, Arnie. Guess where I am?"

"Um, I don't know," I say. "The barn?"

"Nope. The garden. I'm digging potatoes."

I smile as I imagine her knees covered with dirt and her red hair sticking out from under her straw hat. "What are you going to do with them?" I ask.

"Dad promised French fries."

"Aw, man. I love Dad's French fries."

"I know. I wish you were here. He'll make too many as usual." I hear a tinny *thunk*. She must have just dropped a potato into her metal bucket. "What are you doing?" she asks. "No, wait — let me guess. You're reading."

I roll my eyes. "What can I say? The city library is amazing. It has everything. I can't wait until you visit so you can see it."

"Me too! Except I don't think the library will be the first thing I'll want to see."

"We could go to the zoo."

"Sure." She pauses. "Are you worried about starting school?"

"A little," I say. Then I add with a sigh, "Maybe a lot."

"I'm a little worried, too. Alton School won't be the same without you. Anyway, you'll do great. Just be yourself."

"That's what I'm afraid of," I say. "I'm too quiet. I'll never make any friends."

"You'll make friends, Arnie." I hear a slapping noise, then, "Shoot. Darn mosquitoes."

"Are you wearing light colors?" I ask.

"Oops. I forgot," she says. "I'd better find some repellent. These bugs are on me like you on Dad's pancakes."

I snicker. "Bye, Annabelle." I hang up and put my phone away. Thinking about the farm makes this apartment seem even smaller. I need to get out. I jump off the couch and head for the front door.

I lock the door to our apartment and stand in the hallway, unsure where to go. Our building is four stories, with ten apartments on each of the first three floors. I've never seen the fourth floor, though, and I wonder what it's like.

As I head upstairs, a boy carrying a soccer ball passes me on his way down. He stops when he sees me. "Hey," he says, his brown eyes twinkling. He has dark hair and tan skin. "You're the kid who just moved in. Third floor, apartment three-F?"

"That's right," I answer. I wonder how he knows my apartment number.

"I'm Hector," he says. "I live in apartment four-B."

"I'm Arnie," I say, smiling.

"I saw you moving in the other day. Do you play soccer?" He tosses the ball between his hands.

I shake my head.

"Bummer," he says. "Are you going to Washington Middle School? What grade are you in?"

He seems outgoing, like Annabelle.

"Yep," I answer. "I'll be in seventh grade at Washington."

"Awesome. Me too. Maybe we can walk together."

"That would be great," I say.

"I need to get going," Hector says, "but stop by anytime. Just knock quietly, because

my baby brother might be sleeping." He hops down a couple of steps before turning to me again. "Why are you headed up there, anyway? Are you going to the roof?"

"Um . . . the roof," I say, thinking that sounds like a good idea. "Right."

"Rad. See ya."

"See ya." I wave, but Hector's already hopped down to the third floor and doesn't see me.

Hector. I silently repeat his name a few times, so I'll remember it. He seems nice, and I'm glad someone my own age lives in the building. I climb the rest of the way to the fourth floor, where the stairway ends. I wouldn't mind seeing the roof, but I'm not sure how to get to it.

I walk down the hallway, listening to the muffled sounds seeping through thin doors and walls — people talking, a baby crying, a TV blaring. The layout of this floor is similar to ours, except there's a door at the end with a *Roof Access* sign instead of an apartment number.

The knob turns easily and opens into a dim stairwell. I climb until I reach another door, which squeals as I open it. I have to blink a few times until my eyes adjust to the bright sunlight, and then I step outside.

The roof is flat and painted gray. There are pipes and ducts sticking up here and there. Just to the left of the staircase, someone has placed potted plants and two patio chairs close together. I turn in a circle and look at all the buildings surrounding us. I can see the hospital where Mom works, lots of other office and apartment buildings, and the big park. The view is amazing, and I feel like I can breathe again.

But it sure is noisy outside. Traffic sounds float up from the street, and I hear shouts and laughter. I peer over the short wall that edges the roof. Down below, kids are kicking a soccer ball in the alley between our building and the one next door. I wonder if Hector is part of the group. They look like they're having fun. I wish I could join them, but I'm not brave enough to ask, and anyway, I don't play soccer.

I stand there for several minutes, thinking about the city and about school starting, about Annabelle and Dad on the farm. On my way back to our unit, I glance at apartment four-B and wonder if Hector meant it when he said we should walk to school together. It would be nice to get to know somebody here.

Annabelle

CHAPTER 2

BACK TO SCHOOL

"Hold it still, sweetie," Dad says as he drills holes into a piece of wood. "Do you want to do the honors?" He holds the drill out for me.

"Sure." I put the screw bit into the electric drill. Then I attach screws through the strip of wood into the plywood that I stained dark brown this morning.

It's Sunday, and Dad and I are building a bat house in the barn. We're hoping bats will want to live in it and eat the mosquitoes in our yard. Arnie found a do-it-yourself plan online over the summer, before he and Mom moved. But with Mom and Dad separating and the garden vegetables needing canning, it's taken us a while to get to it.

Dad takes off his cap, tosses it on the counter, and scratches his head. He has curly red hair like mine, but his has been getting thinner lately. "There won't be much room between the front and back," he says. "Are you sure these directions are right?"

"Arnie said bats like tight spaces," I reply. "It makes it warm for their babies."

"Okay. You guys are the experts." He glances at the Adirondack boat he's been building as he reaches for another piece of wood. The boat is only partly done. He hasn't worked on it since he and Mom decided to separate.

"I can keep working on the bat house," I say, "if you want to switch to the boat."

"Hmm?" he murmurs, looking back at me. "Oh, no. That's okay." He smiles, but he doesn't look happy. That's nothing new — he hasn't looked happy since Mom and Arnie left.

My phone dings with a text. "It's from Arnie," I tell Dad.

Arnie writes: School starts tomorrow! I'm going to die.

I write back: No u won't! Remember to breathe. Bat house half done.

Arnie: Awesome. Hector's teaching me to play soccer today.

Me: Soccer?

Arnie: I can't wait for you to meet him. I'd better go. See ya.

Me: C ya.

I'm really glad Arnie has found a friend already. We have been calling and texting a few times a day since Mom got us these phones, which is how I know about Hector. But soccer? I laugh out loud, because my brother has never been interested in team sports.

* * *

I ride my bike to school on my first day of sixth grade. It feels strange riding alone, without Arnie.

Usually I love summer vacation and never want it to end. But since Mom and Arnie left, it's just been me and Dad rattling around in our big old farmhouse, and I've started feeling lonely. My best friend, Melody, was at horse camp for most of the summer, and I haven't seen her since June. I'm looking forward to hanging out with her and my other friends again.

I park my bike at the rack and walk to Mr. Swanson's room. He's the sixth-grade teacher and taught Arnie last year. Our school is small, and we only switch classrooms for math and foreign language. Arnie liked Mr. Swanson. But Arnie liking a teacher doesn't say much. He likes all his teachers. That's probably because all of his teachers like him. He's always the smartest kid in class and answers the hard questions when no one else raises their hand.

Mr. Swanson is writing on the board when I walk into the classroom. He turns around and smiles when he sees me. "Annabelle, isn't it?" he says. "Arnie Beeler's sister?" I nod, and he continues, "He's an excellent student. I'm sure Mrs. Wilcox will enjoy having him this year."

I choose a seat in the row closest to the windows, since I like looking outside more than I like paying attention to lessons. "Actually, Arnie doesn't go to school here anymore," I say.

"Really?" Mr. Swanson says.

By now, several other students have wandered into the classroom.

"Why doesn't your brother go to school here?" a boy named Theodore asks.

"Because . . . he moved," I say.

"Why didn't you move with him?" asks a girl named Vicki.

"Because . . ." I trail off. I don't want to talk about this. Tears pool in my eyes and I bite my lip, trying not to cry.

"Students," Mr. Swanson says, "find your desks and take a seat. The bell is about to ring."

Biting my lip doesn't work. I face the window to hide my wet cheeks and my quivering chin. Someone slips a tissue onto my desk.

"What's wrong with Annabelle?" a girl whispers.

"I don't know," comes another voice. "Something about her brother. I think he's sick?"

"Did you say her brother *died*?" someone asks.

"My parents separated!" I blurt out. "Arnie is living with my mom in the city. I'm staying here with my dad. Are you happy now?"

I jump up, run to the restroom, and hide in a stall. I'd planned on telling Melody, but I didn't think I'd have to tell the entire class. This is too hard. I want to go home.

After a few minutes, the door to the restroom opens and someone comes in. "Annabelle?" a woman says softly. "Mr. Swanson called me. Are you okay?"

I recognize her voice. It's Mrs. Johar, the guidance counselor. She sounds so caring, it makes me cry harder. I hear the faucet running. Then she hands me a dampened paper towel under the stall. I wipe my eyes and face.

"I know Arnie isn't enrolled here this year, but I don't know why," she says.

"My parents separated," I say. "Arnie moved away with my mom."

She sighs. "I'm sorry. I know how hard that can be. My parents separated when I was about your age."

"Did you ever get over it?" I ask, sniffling, as I walk out of the stall.

She smiles encouragingly. "In some ways, no. But in most ways, yes." She pats my shoulder. "Do you want to come sit in my office for a while?"

I've finally stopped crying. "No, I'm fine. I should go back to class."

"Let me know if you need anything, okay?"

"Thanks," I say. I wait another minute or two, until my eyes aren't so red, and then I return to class. Everyone stares at me, including Melody, who's sitting at the desk beside mine. *You okay?* she mouths.

I nod and try to smile.

I was so worried about Arnie starting his new school, but I guess I should have been more worried about myself.

Arnie

CHAPTER 3
FIRST DAY BLUES

Mom took me to Washington Middle School right after we moved to the city. I met the school secretary and Mrs. Tsing, the principal. She had a friendly smile and seemed very nice. "How many students were at your old school?" she asked me.

"About a hundred and fifty," I answered.

She chuckled. "You'll find it quite different here. We have over seven hundred students in sixth through eighth grades."

"Alton School was kindergarten through eighth!" I said in disbelief.

She looked through my grades and test scores. "It seems you qualify for advanced English and math. Want me to sign you up for those classes?"

"Sure!" I answered.

Later, Mom said, "Think how fun it will be to go to a school where you can take special classes and all the kids are around your age."

I think about the second part of what Mom said as I walk with Hector to school on Monday. Seven hundred kids between the ages of eleven and fourteen, all in one place. It's a little overwhelming.

Hector bounces his soccer ball as we walk. "My favorite team is the Panama National Team, because my family is from Panama. A lot of my relatives live there. Their team is rad, but I like players from a bunch of different countries."

"I really want to learn more about soccer," I say. "I think I'll get some books on it from the library."

Hector smirks. "Reading about soccer won't help you much. The best way to learn is to just play it."

"Right." I can't help smiling. Hector just reminded me of Annabelle again, the way he likes to do things instead of study things.

Yesterday, Hector taught me some soccer moves. It was fun. I like to run, and soccer has lots of running. I think I'll borrow some books at the library anyway, so I can at least learn about the rules and history.

I'm grateful to be walking with Hector this morning. All this talk about soccer is distracting me from how nervous I am.

A block away, I see kids streaming up the steps of the two-story school.

As we get closer, Hector waves at a boy who runs over and joins us. "Hey, Garza!" he says. They bump fists. "This is Arnie."

"Hi," the boy says. "I'm Emile."

"Call him Garza," Hector says. "Everyone else does."

"Hi," I say.

"So what's your schedule like?" Garza asks Hector. They pull out their schedules and compare them. Hector and I did the same thing yesterday and found out we have two classes together — fourth-period science and sixth-period social studies.

"First period together — yes!" Garza says. "Let's go, before all the seats in back are taken."

"See you later, Arnie!" Hector says with a wave, and the two of them take off.

"See ya," I say, suddenly feeling lost. My first class is algebra, room one thirty-seven, but I have no idea where to find it.

I walk slowly up the cement steps. The noise seems to increase a million decibels once I'm inside, with kids talking, shouting, and laughing. The hallway splits in two directions, left and right. In front of me, a wide staircase leads to the second floor and downstairs. Kids run and bump into me, even though the hall monitors keep shouting, "No running!"

I'm guessing room one thirty-seven is on the first floor of the building. But should I go left or right? Two girls walk by, talking to each other excitedly.

"Excuse me," I say. "Can you tell me where room one thirty-seven is?"

They keep talking and ignore me. I end up asking one of the hall monitors. He points to the left. "Better hurry," he says. "The bell's about to ring."

"Thanks," I say as I take off down the hallway. By the time I find my classroom, the halls are mostly empty. I step inside, my heart pounding. There are only two empty seats. I quickly slide into the one closest to the front. The teacher glares at everyone and crosses her arms over her chest.

Oh, man. What a morning. Compared to this, Annabelle has it so easy at Alton. The bell hasn't rung yet, so I pull my phone out of my backpack to text her.

"No cell phones!" the teacher yells, her eyes shooting darts at me. "You know the rules!"

The kids around me snicker.

"Sorry," I say, and I quickly put it away.

*   *   *

There are only five minutes between periods, so I have to rush to find all of my classes. I make it to fourth-period science just as the bell rings, and I search for a seat.

"Arnie!" Hector waves from the back of the room. I gladly scoot into the desk he's saved for me.

Class isn't very interesting. Like my other teachers, Ms. Hughes spends most of the period reviewing last year, going over the coming year, and explaining what she expects from us. Then the bell rings and it's time for lunch.

"There are three lunch periods," Hector explains as we make our way through the crowded corridor. "Sixth grade goes first, then seventh, and then eighth." We join the river of seventh graders flowing downstairs to the cafeteria.

I didn't bring my lunch, so Hector points me in the direction of the food line. "Our table is in the back, over there." He waves toward zillions of tables and noisy kids. "We all pack our lunches, since it takes so long to get through the line."

I head to the line, which does take forever, just like Hector said it would. When I finally get my food, I look around for him, but by the time I spot him he's already going outside with his friends.

I find an empty table in a dim corner and eat my meaty macaroni. At least I finally have a chance to check my phone.

I have a text from Annabelle: Having a terrible day. Wish you were here.

I text back: Same here.

Annabelle

CHAPTER 4

A NEW FRIEND

Melody is the only person who sits with me in the cafeteria at lunch. She talks nonstop about her summer camp and the horses she rode and fell in love with. I'm glad she's not asking questions about my family, but I also wish she cared enough to want to know what happened.

After three months of summer, I'm not used to being cooped up all day. "Do you want to go outside?" I ask when we finish eating. We usually walk around the playground when the weather is nice.

"No, I think I'll stay inside," she says. "I promised Vicki and Shelly I'd tell them about horse camp."

"Okay. I'm going out," I say. "See you later."

As I leave the lunchroom, Melody gets up from our table and sits with Vicki and Shelly. They're my friends too, but they seem like strangers today. I wonder why they didn't sit with Melody and me before. Are they embarrassed because I cried in class? Do they think what happened to my parents is contagious, like if they get too close to me, their parents will separate too?

I sit on a bench outside and watch kids play basketball. I text Arnie about my terrible day. I hope his is better.

"Hi. Is it okay if I sit with you?"

I look up and see Jayla. She started at Alton School midway through last school year. She's smart and quiet and really good at math, but she hasn't totally fit in yet.

"Hi," I say.

"I heard what you said in class this morning," she says. "My parents separated, too."

"Really?"

She nods. "They split up when I was ten. That's when I moved to Alton with my mom."

"Do you have brothers or sisters?" I ask.

"Nope, just me."

"Then you're kind of lucky. I miss my mom *and* my brother."

"I miss my dad," she says. "And my best friend. And my fish."

"Fish?"

Her eyes light up. "Saltwater — clown fish, angel fish, tangs, a bunch more. They're beautiful. My dad takes care of them, so he kept the aquarium."

I snicker. "You remind me of my brother. He's really into birds."

"Does he have any as pets?"

"No, but he likes seeing them in nature. He and my mom are birders."

"That's cool."

"Yeah. I'll be visiting them for the first time the weekend after next. I can't wait."

"I love visiting my dad," Jayla says. "I go every other weekend. And I stayed with him over the summer for a month."

"Did your parents . . . get divorced?" I ask cautiously.

"Yes," Jayla says quietly.

Now I wish I hadn't asked. I'm still hoping that Mom and Dad will get back together, and I don't want to think about the possibility of them getting divorced. I look at the ground and scuff my shoes on the asphalt. "I hate this. I hate all of it."

"Me too," she says. "But I'm a little more used to it now."

*　*　*

The final bell rings. "So I guess I'll see you tomorrow," I say to Melody. She lives close to school and walks home.

"Okay," she says. "See ya."

"Hey," I say, remembering an assignment Mr. Swanson gave us earlier. "Do you want to work on that social studies project together? You can come over this weekend, and we can get started. Plus you can see the bat house my dad and I are making."

She pauses. "I don't know. I'll have to check." She waves. "Bye!"

Vicki and Shelly are waiting for her outside, and they walk together.

I ride my bike home, thinking about Melody. She always liked visiting the farm.

My cell phone rings, and I stop under a tree and pull the phone out of my backpack. Arnie's name pops up on the screen.

"Hi!" I answer.

"Hi," he says. "So, what was so terrible about your day?"

I tell him about shouting to the whole class that our parents had separated. I also tell him about how Melody is acting strangely.

He tells me about his huge new school. "I felt lost, Annabelle," he says. "I miss Alton. I miss my old friends. I miss riding my bike."

"What about your new friend, Hector?" I ask.

"He already has friends."

"I'm sure he won't mind if you hang out with them. Stop worrying and just do it."

"Just do it," he repeats. "Hector would probably say the same thing. You guys are a lot alike."

"That's funny," I say. "I got to know someone today who reminds me of you. Do you remember Jayla, the girl who moved here last year? She likes fish, almost as much as you like birds. And she likes to read."

"Oh yeah?" Arnie says.

"Her parents aren't together anymore either," I say, "so we had a lot to talk about at lunch today."

He doesn't say anything.

"Arnie, are you still there?"

"Yes." He sighs. "It's just . . . sometimes I get tired of all this change, and I wish things would go back to how they used to be."

"Me too," I say with a sigh of my own.

I hear knocking.

"Wait a sec," Arnie says. "Someone's at the door."

I hear the door squeak and then a boy's voice. "Wanna kick the soccer ball around?"

"Sure!" I hear Arnie say. Then into the phone, he says, "Hector's here. Gotta go."

"Okay, bye," I say. "Talk to you later?"

But Arnie doesn't answer. He's already ended the call.

Arnie

CHAPTER 5

ARNIPEDIA

On Monday night, Mom works late and brings Chinese takeout home for dinner. There's no Chinese restaurant anywhere near Alton, so it's a real treat. I dish the fried rice, beef-broccoli, and almond-chicken out of the little boxes. The food is so delicious, I feel like I could eat it all, but I'm trying to save some for leftovers.

"I want to start taking my lunch instead of buying," I tell Mom.

"Why? Is the cafeteria food that terrible?"

"No, it's fine. But Hector and his friends bring their lunches, and I want to eat with them."

"Okay, then. I'll pick up some deli meats at the market," Mom says.

"I'll take leftovers tomorrow."

After I tell Mom about my first day at school, she reminds me that Annabelle is visiting soon. "We need to talk about the weekend after next," she says, "and decide what we're going to do when your sister is here."

"I think she might want to go to the zoo."

"All right. Anything else? She hasn't mentioned anything to me."

I shake my head. Mom has spoken to Annabelle a few times since we left the farm.

But nothing like all the texts and calls my sister and I have been making. I wonder if I should mention what happened to Annabelle on her first day of school, but then I quickly decide against it. I think it's up to Annabelle to decide what she tells Mom.

I help clean the dishes, then tell Mom I'm going up to Hector's apartment to do homework. But instead of going to Hector's, I climb the stairs to the roof. I'm not sure why I lied; it's not something I usually do. Maybe it's because I want to keep the roof to myself — my own private place — even though I know that's a dumb idea. Looking at the potted plants and chairs, it's clear that other people come up here too.

The sun has just set and the sky glows a faint red. There are too many city lights to see the stars, but I know they're up there somewhere. I only stay for a few minutes —

just long enough to feel a little less cramped and to remind myself of the farm. I wonder what Annabelle and Dad are doing. I wonder if they're thinking about me.

* * *

The next day, I find all of my classes without any problem. I choose desks near the front, except in the two classes I have with Hector. In those classes, we pick seats in the back, where he likes to sit. After fourth period, Hector and I walk to the cafeteria together. Sitting at Hector's table are Garza and some of his other friends — Amar, TJ, and Levi. I feel nervous, like I'm barging in. But I think about what Annabelle said — just do it.

I only listen at first, while they talk about things I don't know much about — soccer and girls they like. But when TJ starts talking about his uncle who keeps homing pigeons on the roof of his apartment building, I can't help jumping in.

"That's awesome!" I say.

They stare at me. My cheeks heat up.

"You like pigeons?" TJ asks.

"Um . . . I like all birds," I answer. "Did you know that homing pigeons were used as messengers during wars, before there were phones or telegraphs? There's a theory that they map their surroundings using sound waves. Or it could be that they find their way home by smell or by magnetic fields."

Amar smirks and says, "What are you, a walking Wikipedia?"

"No, he's Arnipedia," Hector says, grinning.

"Hah!" TJ laughs. "Arnipedia."

"Too long," says Levi. "What about Arnipede? You know, like centipede?"

"Arnie Peed?" Garza says. Everyone cracks up, including Hector.

I smile and try to laugh along with them, but I'm really hoping Arnie Peed doesn't stick.

"Come on," Hector says. "Let's go, before lunch ends."

I hang back a little as I follow them upstairs to the rear of the building. We step outside and onto a playground I haven't seen before — a rectangle of asphalt. Hector drops his soccer ball and kicks it to Garza, who kicks it to TJ. The five of them run ahead, chasing the ball. I've been laughed at enough today, so I shove my hands into my pockets and watch.

"Come on, Arnie!" Hector calls. "Three on three."

I'm about to shake my head, but then I hear Annabelle's *just do it* in my mind again, and I jump into the game.

Every day after school over the next two weeks, Hector and I go down to the alley and he teaches me soccer moves. Sometimes other kids are there, but sometimes it's just us two.

On the Thursday before Annabelle arrives, Hector and I are walking back to our apartment building after our practice. "You have a lot of stamina and long legs," he says. "You'd make a rad midfielder."

Midfielders cover a lot of ground. They play both offense and defense. I know this from the soccer books I've been reading.

"Our school team could use another midfielder," Hector says. "You should try out."

"Really?" I say. It's never occurred to me to play on a team.

"Second semester. Practices start in February."

"Is that why you've been teaching me?" I ask. "Because you need another midfielder?"

"Partly." He grins. "Hey, do you want to come up to my place for dinner? My parents said you're welcome to. And, uh, maybe you could help me a little with my math homework? Ms. Peters is the hardest math teacher in the whole school."

"Sure. That would be great," I say as we walk to our building. After I call Mom and get her okay, Hector and I race up the four flights of stairs to his apartment.

It's time for bed by the time I get home from Hector's. I helped him with his homework the same way I used to help Annabelle. Thinking about Annabelle, I realize we haven't spoken since yesterday, and we only texted once on Wednesday. I check my phone and there are no texts or voicemails from her. I sigh and turn my phone off.

Annabelle

CHAPTER 6
OUTSIDER

It's Friday after school, and Dad and I are sitting in the van, which is still parked in the driveway. He taps the steering wheel. "Toothbrush?" he asks.

"Yes."

"Toothpaste? Pajamas?"

"Ditto."

"What about your phone?"

"Got it."

"Oh, money!" He pulls his wallet out of his pocket and hands me two twenty-dollar bills.

"Thanks," I say, "but I'll be staying with Mom, so I don't think I'll need to buy anything."

"You should never be in a city without cash, in case you need to take a cab or there's some kind of emergency. And remember, you can call me if you need anything. I won't be going anywhere this weekend — just sticking around here at the farm."

"Dad, I'll be fine," I say. I'm starting to get antsy. "Um, do you think we should get going?"

He sighs. "Right." He starts the engine and drives slowly down the driveway. "I'm sorry for being such a mother hen," he says. "I'm going to miss you."

I look over at him. His eyes glisten, like he's about to cry. "Are *you* going to be okay?" I ask.

He sits up straighter as he pulls out onto the main road. "Of course. I have the boat to keep me busy. And the bookcase Jack Todd hired me to build. I really need to get going on that."

We pass Alton School on our way to the highway. Last week, Melody said she couldn't come to the farm. She also said Vicki was feeling insecure about the social studies project, so Melody agreed to work with her on it.

"I hope you understand," Melody said.

"Sure," I said, even though I didn't really understand.

But instead of stewing about it, I decided to ask Jayla if she wanted to work on the project with me. She agreed and came to the farm last Saturday. She was amazed by everything — the garden, the barn, our old house, Dad's workshop. We decided to do our project on ancient Egypt. I'm planning to make a pyramid out of wood scraps, and Jayla has already started researching for the report. I really like Jayla, but I miss the way things used to be with Melody. I wish I knew what to do about it.

I stare out the van's passenger window as we drive and watch as forests, houses, and fields fly by. Eventually the fields turn into suburbs, and the tall buildings of the city come into view. I start to bite my lip and tap my feet. I haven't seen Mom and Arnie in over three weeks. *Have they changed?* I wonder. *Will they think I've changed?*

The traffic is terrible, and we keep getting turned around on one-way streets. I can't help but stare at the buildings and pedestrians.

It's amazing to think my brother and mom actually live here, right in the middle of this big city.

We finally get to the address Mom gave us. There aren't any open parking spaces, so Dad has to pull over in front of a fire hydrant. I text Arnie: We're here!

He texts back: Be right down!

Dad and I get out of the car, and he gives me a big hug. "I love you, Annabelle. I'll be here Sunday to pick you up." He lets me go and glances up at the building. "I can't wait to hear all about Arnie and . . . your adventures."

I think he was about to mention Mom. "I love you too, Dad," I say. "See you on Sunday."

The front door of the apartment building opens, and Arnie trots down the steps. "Hi,

Annabelle. Hi, Dad." Dad and Arnie hug, and I stand out of the way while they talk. A few minutes later, Dad says, "Guess I'd better be going. Don't want to get a ticket."

He glances up at the building again. I secretly hope Mom is standing by one of those windows, looking down at him. I hope they see each other and remember the connection they once had.

"Well," Dad says with a sigh, looking at us again. "Have fun, kids."

I feel so sad for him as he climbs into the van that I almost want to home with him. Like Arnie said, sometimes I'm okay with all of this change, and other times I'm just sick of it.

We wave as he drives off. Arnie and I look at each other and smile.

"You look the same," I say.

"Of course I do! It's only been three weeks. Let's go upstairs. I have so much to tell you!"

He takes off, hoisting my backpack over his shoulder. By the time we get to the third floor, I'm panting, but Arnie isn't winded at all. "You're in good shape," I say.

"I'm used to the stairs now. They're good exercise. Playing soccer probably helps too."

"I still can't believe you're playing soccer."

"I know, it's crazy," Arnie says. "Well, not literally crazy, but —"

I roll my eyes and snicker. "I know what you mean."

When we get to apartment three-F, the door opens in front of us, and Mom and I hug each other tightly. She's crying, and I wonder if she's thinking about the day she and Arnie left Alton for the city — about how I didn't say goodbye. We've spoken on the phone since then, but it's not the same as seeing each other face to face.

She finally lets me go. "I'm so happy to see you," she says, stroking my hair and staring at me as if she's not sure I'm really here. "Have you eaten?"

I shake my head.

"Then you must be hungry." She hurries into the kitchen, which is separated from the living room by a small counter.

"Do you cook now?" I ask. At the farm, Dad made all of our meals.

"Of course!" she says. "Well, let's say I buy things and heat them up. But I'm quite handy chopping vegetables for salads, aren't I, Arnie?"

"Yep," Arnie says.

They smile at each other as though they're sharing a private joke, and I suddenly feel like I'm on the outside looking in.

Arnie

CHAPTER 7

SIGHTSEEING AND SUNDAES

I can't help but wish Dad were here. But being with three-quarters of my family is better than only being with half.

I give my sister a tour of our place while Mom heats stew and makes a salad. The tour only takes a minute. I watch Annabelle as she takes in the tiny apartment. She makes polite comments, like, "That's a really nice view," and, "The carpet is so soft," but I bet she's comparing it to the farmhouse, like I did when we first moved in.

"How much longer until dinner?" I ask Mom. "Can I take Annabelle up to meet Hector?"

"Okay. Be back in fifteen minutes."

Annabelle lags behind as we climb the stairs to the fourth floor. I stop and wait for her. The grumpy expression on her face tells me she's either tired or wishing she were doing something else.

"Sorry, Annabelle," I say. "I just really want you to meet Hector. I know you're going to like him. He's rad."

"Rad?" she says with a smirk. "I've never heard you say that before."

"I probably picked it up from Hector. It means radical."

"Yeah, I figured."

We walk down the hall, and I knock softly on Hector's door. "He has a baby brother," I whisper. "He screams like crazy if you wake him from a nap."

Hector's dad opens the door. I've met him a few times. He's short and a little overweight and he always has a big smile on his face. "Arnie! Come in."

We step inside. "Is Hector home?" I ask.

"Hector!" his dad yells into the apartment, which is much bigger than ours. I guess that means baby Diego isn't sleeping. A few seconds later, Hector emerges from one of the bedrooms.

"Hey, Hector!" I say. "This is my sister, Annabelle."

Hector smiles and sticks his hand out. "Hi."

Annabelle shakes his hand. "Hi." She holds back a little, like she's feeling shy — which is strange, because my sister is never shy.

"Do you play soccer?" Hector asks.

"No," Annabelle says, narrowing her eyes. "Should I?"

"It's no big deal," Hector says. "I ask everybody that question. Don't I, Arnie?"

"Yeah, it's pretty annoying," I joke, and we both laugh. "Well, I just wanted you to meet each other. I've been telling Hector all about you, Annabelle."

"He totally has," Hector says. "Talk about annoying."

"So can you hang out with us tomorrow?" I ask him.

"I wish. But I have to babysit." He makes a face.

"Darn. Well, our mom's making dinner now, so we'd better get going. Maybe we'll catch up with you on Sunday."

"Rad," Hector says as we walk out to the hallway. "See ya later."

I notice Annabelle is super quiet as we make our way down to the third floor.

"What's wrong, Annabelle?" I ask. "I thought you'd like Hector."

She shrugs. "I just met him. I don't have an opinion yet."

"Why are you acting so strange? You're usually really friendly."

She hesitates before answering, "I'm just tired."

We get to the apartment, and I set out plates. Then we sit at the counter and eat stew, salad, and French bread. Mom asks Annabelle about school, but she doesn't ask many questions about the farm, and she doesn't ask a thing about Dad.

Annabelle only perks up when she talks about her new friend, Jayla. Jayla likes saltwater fish. Jayla likes going to the library. Jayla is crazy about Annabelle's vegetable garden. Mom nods and smiles.

"She's really cool, Mom," Annabelle says. "Oh, and Jayla's parents aren't together either, so she completely understands what I'm going through."

Mom looks down at her plate and lowers her fork. What Annabelle just said obviously bothers her, but Annabelle keeps eating and doesn't seem to notice.

Mom pushes away from the counter and clears her plate. "So, who wants hot-fudge sundaes?" she asks from the kitchen.

"I do!" Annabelle says.

"Me too," I say. "Wait until you try this fudge sauce, Annabelle. We get it from a little Greek grocery store down the street. It's really good."

"It can't be better than the homemade kind we buy at the Alton farmer's market."

"Yeah, it is. You'll see."

I start doing the dishes while Mom fixes dessert. Annabelle digs into her sundae as soon as Mom sets it on the counter.

"Well?" I say, smiling. "I told you."

She shrugs. "It's okay. But not as good as the kind from Alton."

*   *   *

We've barely finished breakfast Saturday morning when Mom scoots us out the door. The three of us spend all day sightseeing. We go to the park and the zoo. Then we visit the natural history museum.

I wish Hector could have come with us. There are things I know he'd enjoy, like the exhibit at the museum about the history of sports. We learn about an Aztec hoop game that had a rule that players couldn't touch the ball with their hands. Kind of like soccer, except the ball couldn't touch the ground either. And the leader of the losing team was sometimes sacrificed. Talk about pressure to win.

I wish I knew what's wrong with Annabelle. She's been quiet all day. I talk to her and ask her questions, but she doesn't say much in return. I can't help but wonder if she'd rather be spending the day in Alton with her new friend Jayla.

Annabelle

CHAPTER 8
LEFT OUT

We've just left the natural history museum.
Mom said something about visiting the
hospital where she works on our way to the
apartment. It already feels like we've walked
from one end of the city to the other. I just
want to be in the apartment with Mom and
Arnie so I can get to know my new second
home. I brought some clothes and pajamas
with me to keep there, and I don't even know
where to put them.

From what Arnie said, I thought the apartment would be terrible — no room to even walk around. But it's cozy and cute, with lots of light streaming through the windows. The pullout couch is comfortable enough, and last night I fell asleep right away.

My feet hurt, and I lag behind, watching Arnie and Mom walk together ahead of me. They've always been close, but now it feels like I don't know either of them anymore . . . especially Arnie. In just three weeks, he's changed so much — the words he uses, the things he does. Mom just seems distracted. I don't like seeing them in this new place, and I feel like I don't belong. I think about calling Dad and asking him to pick me up early.

Mom and Arnie finally stop walking and wait for me.

"You look tired," Mom says.

I nod.

"Want to go home?"

At first I think she means the farm, and I start to panic. Is she sick of me already? Does she want me to leave? Then I realize she's talking about the apartment. "Yes," I say. "That would be nice."

"Maybe I can show you the hospital tomorrow." She checks her watch. "It's almost time for dinner anyway. Pizza or Chinese?"

"Pizza!" Arnie shouts. "Let's go to Luigi's."

"How far is it?" I ask, dreading the idea of more walking.

"Just down the street from our apartment," he says. "It's the place I told you about when we first moved. We went with Bill and Jerry."

"Who are Bill and Jerry?" I ask.

"Friends from the hospital," Mom says. "They helped us move in."

"Oh, right. I forgot." My head hurts as much as my feet, trying to keep track of everything.

Luigi's is hectic and loud, and Mom and Arnie insist on getting plain cheese pizza. They say it's the most authentic. We sit at a small table, and Mom and Arnie fold their huge slices in half before they eat, so I do the same thing. It tastes good, but I miss pepperoni.

Arnie leans back in his chair and smiles. He looks so comfortable, you'd think he's been eating at Luigi's all his life. Meanwhile, the guys behind the counter scream at the cooks and the customers, who all scream back at them.

"Maybe we can hang out with Hector when we get back," Arnie says.

"NO!" I yell. I'm instantly embarrassed. Why did I shout? Luckily the only people who

seem to have noticed are Mom and Arnie, who stare at me. "I just want to be with you guys!" I toss my pizza slice onto my plate and run out of the restaurant.

If I were at the farm, I'd go to the garden or the barn, someplace I could be alone and calm down. Here, I'm surrounded by cars, strangers, and tall buildings, and I don't know my way around.

Arnie comes outside a minute later and bumps my shoulder with his, while Mom lingers a few feet behind us. "Come on," he says. "Let's go."

"Where are we going now?" I ask, fighting back tears.

"Home, of course."

He leads the way, and Mom and I follow him down the block. She wraps her arm around me.

She's quiet for a moment, then says, "I'm sorry if we did too much today." She takes a deep breath. "I've missed you so much, Annabelle. Do you know I was nervous about this weekend?"

I shake my head.

"I wanted everything to be perfect for you. I wanted you to have fun, not be cooped up in that small apartment. I think more than anything, I wanted . . . I wanted you to like me again."

"I like you," I say.

"But it's not the same as before. I know you're angry that I moved out and that Arnie came with me," she says. "I'm glad you have a new friend you can talk to who's gone through something similar. I'm just sorry you can't talk to me. I'm your mom, and I want that to be my job."

We've reached the front of the apartment building. She squeezes my shoulder and says, "It feels as though I'm on the outside of your life looking in. That's a sad and uncomfortable place to be. Does that make sense?"

"Yes." I don't tell her I've been feeling the exact same way about her and Arnie.

Arnie is standing on the top step, holding the front door open for us.

Mom grabs my hand before I go in. "I know it may take some time," she says softly, "but I hope you'll let me in again."

I hug her and nod. Then I begin to cry. "I think Melody's not my best friend anymore."

"Oh, sweetie." Mom hugs me tightly. "I'm so sorry. Friendships often change at your age. But the timing couldn't be worse, could it?"

I shake my head and walk into the building, sobbing. I wish there was a private place I could cry, but I guess the bathroom will have to do.

Arnie

CHAPTER 9

HOMESICK

Annabelle walks past me into the apartment and straight to the bathroom, slamming the door behind her. I don't know what she and Mom were talking about, but Annabelle got really upset at Luigi's when I mentioned hanging out with Hector tonight. I was so certain she would like him as much as I do.

Annabelle has changed. She used to be brave and full of adventure, always wanting to go places and meet new people. Now she seems shy and uncertain.

She's in the bathroom for a long time. I don't want to bother her, but I really have to go.

"Mom," I say, poking my head into her bedroom. "Can I go up to Hector's to use their bathroom?"

"Go ahead," she answers. She's sitting on her bed, and her eyes look red, as if she's been crying too.

I head up to Hector's. He answers the door with a smile. It's nice to see a happy face. "Can I use your bathroom?" I ask. "Annabelle is hiding out in ours."

He rolls his eyes. "Sisters."

I use their bathroom and then walk down the hall to Hector's room, which he shares with his younger brother, Lucas. They're both in there, building a Lego house.

"Do you think girls are more emotional than boys?" I ask.

"Definitely," Hector says. "You should see my mom and sister. Total waterworks, man."

"I should do some research," I say. "Find out if it's true."

Hector laughs. "You crack me up, Arnie. You really are an Arnipedia."

"What's that?" Lucas asks.

"Someone who knows a lot of stuff and is named Arnie," Hector says. Then he looks at me. "Want to help with our building project?"

"Not tonight, but thanks," I say. "Maybe tomorrow."

I say goodbye to Hector and Lucas and stand in the hallway outside their apartment. I'd planned on going straight home. Annabelle is only here for the weekend, and it doesn't seem fair to stay away too long. But then again, being around me seems to be making her sad, and she's probably still in the bathroom anyway.

I decide to head up to the roof for a few minutes.

An elderly man and woman are sitting in the patio chairs. I recognize them from a couple of days ago, when Hector introduced me to them and they showed me their plants. "Hi, Mr. and Mrs. Schultz," I say.

"Hello, Arnie," Mrs. Schultz says.

I notice they've pruned a tree. "The ficus looks nice," I say.

"Yep, it was getting leggy," Mr. Schultz says. "Nice evening, isn't it? Look at that moon."

I look up and see that the moon is almost full. I stare at it for a minute, wondering what it would look like from the farm. "Well, see you later," I say with a sigh as I head back toward the staircase.

"Enjoy your evening," Mrs. Schultz says.

By the time I get back to the apartment, Mom and Annabelle are on the couch, watching a movie on TV. Annabelle is snuggled up against Mom, who has her arm around her. I'm glad they're not fighting or crying anymore.

I sit down next to Annabelle. "What are you watching?" I ask.

Annabelle doesn't answer.

"An old Western," Mom says.

"Is it any good?"

"Shh!" Annabelle hisses sharply.

"What? I was just asking."

Annabelle doesn't look at me. She hardly says a word to me for the rest of the night.

*   *   *

"Shall we go out to breakfast?" Mom asks.
It's Sunday morning, and Dad will be picking
up Annabelle this afternoon.

"Can't we stay here?" Annabelle asks.
She flits around the small kitchen, searching
through the cupboards and the refrigerator.
"I feel like pancakes, and you have all the
ingredients."

"Pancakes?" Mom says a little nervously.
"I've never made them from scratch before."

"I know how," Annabelle says. "I'll do it."

"Well, okay," Mom replies. "Sounds good to
me."

I drink orange juice at the counter and
watch my sister. For the first time since she got
here, she acts like she's comfortable. I think I
understand why. Annabelle is always happiest
when she's making something.

The pancakes are delicious — almost as good as Dad's. For a minute it feels like I'm back at the farmhouse, sitting at the big wooden table and listening to Dad humming while he cooks. I imagine all of us talking about our plans for the day — maybe going to the lake together or doing our own things. I picture Annabelle working in the garden, Mom sitting on the porch and talking to Grandma Sophie on the phone, Dad working on one of his projects in the barn. I imagine riding my bike to the library and borrowing books I've already read ten times, and then reading them again in my room. My big, quiet room.

I suddenly feel so homesick I can't eat. I miss home. I miss Dad. I miss Annabelle. I miss my old school. I've been so busy getting used to my new life, I've pushed my old life away.

Hector is nice, but my old friend, Jeremy, knows me better. Soccer is okay, but I'd rather jog along the old forest road with Mom than kick a soccer ball in a dirty alley. Washington Middle School is close enough that I can walk there, but it's big, and most of the students are unfriendly, and the teachers don't know me. The library here has every kind of book you can imagine, but the librarians will never learn my name and hold books aside for me like Mrs. Norris did at the library in Alton.

I've been acting as though my old life never happened. Except it did. And I want it back.

"Honey, are you all right?" Mom asks.

For the first time since she and Dad split up, I feel anger. Red, fiery anger. "No," I say, "I'm not all right." I don't dare look at her, because I blame her for taking me away.

I can't stay here. I run out of the apartment and race upstairs.

Annabelle

CHAPTER 10

RUNAWAY BROTHER

One second, Arnie is eating pancakes. The next, his entire face turns red and he storms out the door.

"Arnie!" Mom calls.

But he's already gone.

"What was that all about?" I ask.

"I haven't the slightest idea," Mom says. She jumps up from the counter and reaches for her keys.

"Wait, I'll call him." I press his number, but his phone rings next to the couch. He didn't take it with him. I look at Mom. "Maybe we should leave him alone. He's pretty good at figuring things out on his own."

Mom's forehead creases with worry. "I don't know," she says. "I hope he doesn't wander too far. I'd feel a lot better if he had his phone."

"Maybe he went to Hector's."

"Or he might have gone to the library or the park," Mom says.

"I'll go up to Hector's and check," I say.

I run up the stairs to the fourth floor and knock on four-B. A young boy answers. He's still wearing his pajamas. "Hi," he says.

"Hi. Is Arnie here?"

"Arnipedia?" he says.

"What?"

Before he can answer, Hector comes to the door. "Hi, Annabelle," he says.

"Hi. I'm looking for my brother."

"He's not here." I must look worried, because he asks, "Is something wrong?"

"He ran out of the apartment all of a sudden," I say. "My brother is not the run-out-of-the-house type. That's more my style." I can't believe I just said that. My face heats up.

Hector grins, two dimples poking into his cheeks. I'd say they're cute dimples. In fact, I'd say Hector is cute. But I don't know if I like him yet. "I'm sure he's okay," he says.

"You're probably right. Well, thanks." I turn to leave.

"Wait a sec." Hector turns to the boy who's now peering around his legs. "Lucas, tell Mom I'll be back in a few minutes."

The boy nods.

Hector closes the door and says, "Follow me. I have a hunch." He walks to the end of the hallway and opens a door. We climb a dim stairwell and step out onto the roof, where a short woman with gray hair is watering a potted plant.

"Hello, Mrs. Schultz," Hector says. "Do you remember Arnie Beeler? He just moved in a few weeks ago, and I'm wondering —"

"Arnie?" she interrupts. "Sure. Sweet boy." She points to the other side of the roof. "He's over there."

All I see are pipes and ducts in the direction she points. Then, near the edge of the roof, I see a square structure with a door that reminds me of a storage shed. Something blue sticks out behind the structure. It's the same color as . . . come to think of it, I don't remember seeing Arnie's blue beanbag chair in the apartment.

"Arnie?" I call. I run past Hector and around the structure.

On the other side, Arnie is sitting in his beanbag chair. Next to the chair is a small outdoor table, and underneath the table is a clear plastic box filled with books. He brought the box from home, too. I remember he'd packed some of his things in it. Arnie has his feet propped up on the short wall that runs around the edge of the roof. His hands are clasped in his lap.

"Annabelle?" His eyes are red and swollen.

"Hey, man," Hector says behind me. "Rad setup."

Arnie lowers his eyes. I know he's embarrassed about crying.

"Well," Hector says, clearing his throat, "mystery solved. See ya later."

"Thanks," I tell Hector.

"Anytime." He gives me a dimpled grin before he leaves.

I sit down and lean against the wall. "I guess you haven't changed as much as I thought. You still need your own private place."

Arnie nods. "Lots of times when I tell Mom I'm going to Hector's, I come up here instead. This is where I was last night, after I used Hector's bathroom." He glances at me then lowers his eyes again. "I've been sitting here thinking about the farm. I want to go back."

"You do?"

"I'm going to talk to Mom," he says. "See if I can ride home with you and Dad this afternoon."

"But I thought you really like it here."

"In some ways I do, but in other ways I don't. It's so hard to fit in."

I gape at him. "But you are fitting in. You've only been here three weeks and you've already made a good friend . . . who I've decided I like, by the way. And you're playing soccer. And you walk around the city like it's your backyard. And last night at Luigi's? That place is crazy, but you seemed right at home."

He slowly smiles. "I really like Luigi's."

"I think you like the whole city, Arnie," I say. "You're homesick now, but it will pass."

"You sound like you don't want me back," he says. "Especially now that you have *Jayla*."

I snicker and kick his beanbag chair. "Don't be stupid. I want you home more than anything. It's lonely without you and Mom. But I think you should stay here, because Mom needs you, and I think the city is a good place for you." I shake my head. "I can't believe I just said that."

"I can't either," he says with a smile.

We sit quietly, lost in our thoughts. For that moment, it's as if nothing has changed at all.

I glance around the sunny roof. "I could grow tomatoes up here, Arnie. And beans and zucchini and —"

"Annabelle . . ." he says as he stands up.

"Just a few pots," I say, standing beside him.

He takes a deep breath. "Maybe." He slaps at his arm. "Shoot. Between the mosquitoes and crops, I might as well be living on the farm."

"Mosquitoes!" I groan. "Arnie, there's got to be someplace on earth they don't live."

"Iceland, actually," he says. "Maybe we can move there someday."

We head back to our apartment, chatting about mosquitoes and other gross insects. I secretly plan to make another bat house for his roof. I think I'll surprise him with it for his birthday.

GLOSSARY

Aztec (AZ-tek) — relating to the Nahuatl-speaking people that founded the Mexican empire before it was conquered by Cortes in the 16th century

contagious (kuhn-TAY-juhs) — spread by direct or indirect contact with an infected person

cooped up (KOOPT uhp) — confined in a small space

dreading (DRED-ing) — fearing or not looking forward to something that you expect to happen in the near future

fiery (FIRE-ee) — very emotional

homesick (HOME-sik) — sad because you are away from your family and home

hunch (HUHNCH) — an idea that is based on a feeling you have and not backed by facts

midfielder (MID-feel-dur) — in soccer, a player who is active toward the middle of the field, often playing both offense and defense

mosquitoes (muh-SKEE-tohs) — small insects that bite animals and humans and suck their blood

pedestrians (puh-DES-tree-uhns) — people who travel on foot

repellent (ri-PEL-uhnt) — a chemical that wards off insects and other pests

stamina (STAM-uh-nuh) — the energy and strength to keep doing something

TALK IT OVER

1. Annabelle met a new friend in Alton, Jayla, whose parents are also separated. Do you think this factor will lead them to be good friends? Discuss why or why not, using examples from the text.

2. Why do you think it takes Arnie a while to realize that he isn't totally happy with his move to the city? Talk about how his attitude changed throughout the story.

3. Mom and Annabelle both feel like they're on the "outside looking in," when it comes to one another's lives. What do you imagine that would feel like?

WRITE IT DOWN

1. How are Arnie and Annabelle's perspectives on the big change their family has gone through different? How are they similar? Use examples from the text.

2. Arnie and Annabelle each make new friends in this book. Write a short essay describing the first time you met one of your good friends.

3. When Arnie runs out of the apartment upset, Annabelle and Mom aren't sure where to find him. Imagine he ends up somewhere besides the rooftop, and write a different ending to this story.

AUTHOR BIO

M. G. Higgins is an award-winning author who has written over eighty fiction and nonfiction books for children and young adults. Her fiction titles range from sports and adventure to fantasy and science fiction, and she especially likes to write about kids dealing with real-life issues. Before becoming a full-time writer, Ms. Higgins worked as a school counselor and had a private counseling practice. When she's not writing, she enjoys hiking and taking photographs in the Arizona desert, where she lives with her husband and two cats.

ILLUSTRATOR BIO

Jo Taylor is a self-taught illustrator, working in the industry for well over ten years. She lives in Gloucestershire, UK, with her computer-obsessed son, sports-coach daughter, and their shaggy French sheepdog, Blue. Jo's home is in beautiful countryside next to the River Severn. All this nature influences her illustrations and gives her somewhere lovely to walk or run with Blue. Jo starts off her illustrations by hand, using pencils, pens, and a splash of paint. She then mixes them all up in her PC, where she adds lots of color and texture to create fresh, bright, colorful designs.